MW00885358

Best Friend TROUBLE

Frances Itani

illustrated by Geneviève Després

ORCA BOOK PUBLISHERS

Library and Archives Canada Cataloguing in Publication

Itani, Frances, 1942-, author
Best friend trouble / Frances Itani ; illustrated by Geneviève Després.

Issued in print and electronic formats.
ISBN 978-1-55469-891-2 (bound).--ISBN 978-1-55469-892-9 (pdf).--
ISBN 978-1-4598-0714-3 (epub)

I. Després, Geneviève, illustrator II. Title.

PS8567.T35B47 2014 jC813'.54 C2013-906732-9 C2013-906733-7

First published in the United States, 2014
Library of Congress Control Number: 2013951372

Summary: After a fight with her best friend, Lizzy, Hanna learns how to see things from another person's perspective.

Orca Book Publishers is dedicated to preserving the environment and has printed this book on Forest Stewardship Council® certified paper.

Orca Book Publishers gratefully acknowledges the support for its publishing programs provided by the following agencies: the Government of Canada through the Canada Book Fund and the Canada Council for the Arts, and the Province of British Columbia through the BC Arts Council and the Book Publishing Tax Credit.

Cover and interior artwork created using watercolor and color pencil.

Cover artwork by Geneviève Després
Design by Chantal Gabriell

Orca Book Publishers
PO Box 5626, Stn. B
Victoria, BC Canada
V8R 6S4

Orca Book Publishers
PO Box 468
Custer, WA USA
98240-0468

www.orcabook.com
Printed and bound in Canada.

17 16 15 14 • 4 3 2 1

For Campbell, Tate and Frances *—FI*

To my best friends *—GD*

When Lizzy threw her ball, it flew up and up, over the fence at the end of Hanna's yard.

"Ha!" Lizzy said. "I bet you can't throw yours that far."

"Oh yes I can," said Hanna. She took a deep breath and threw as hard as she could.

The ball went high into the air but plopped down on the grass before it reached the fence.

"See?" said Lizzy. "I told you so."

Hanna stomped into the house and slammed the door.

No one was in the kitchen, but loud noises were coming from the basement. Hanna found her big brother Josh down there, building birdhouses.

"What's up?" he said. "I thought you were playing with Lizzy in the yard."

"Lizzy!" said Hanna. "Ha!" She sat on the workbench and sighed.

"I thought you two were friends," said Josh.

"Not anymore," said Hanna. "Lizzy brags. She said she could throw the ball farther than I could."

"And did she?"

"She did," said Hanna. "But the sun was in my eyes, so it wasn't fair. She says she can swing higher than I can too."

"Well, can she?" asked Josh.

"No," said Hanna. "She always starts before I have a chance to pump my feet."

"Sounds like best friend trouble to me," said Josh. "Maybe you can pound in a few nails. That will make you feel better." He gave Hanna a hammer, a block of wood and a handful of nails.

Wham! Wham! Wham! Wham!

Hanna pounded the nails into the wood. Josh was right. She did feel a bit better.

She decided to look for her dad.

Her dad was in the living room, practicing for a concert that evening.

Hanna came in to listen. She sighed a long, drawn-out sigh that stretched as long as the note her dad played on his clarinet.

The music stopped.

"I thought you were playing outside with Lizzy," her dad said.

"Not anymore," said Hanna. "Do you know what Lizzy said?"

"No, but I guess you are going to tell me," said her dad.

"She said I'm not allowed to sing in her backyard. But when she's in our yard, she hollers like an old crow."

"I think I've heard crows singing in both yards," said Hanna's dad. "Sounds like best friend trouble to me."

"She's not my best friend," said Hanna. "She's mean and she makes me tired."

"Why don't you dig into the music box?" said her dad. "Choose any instrument you like."

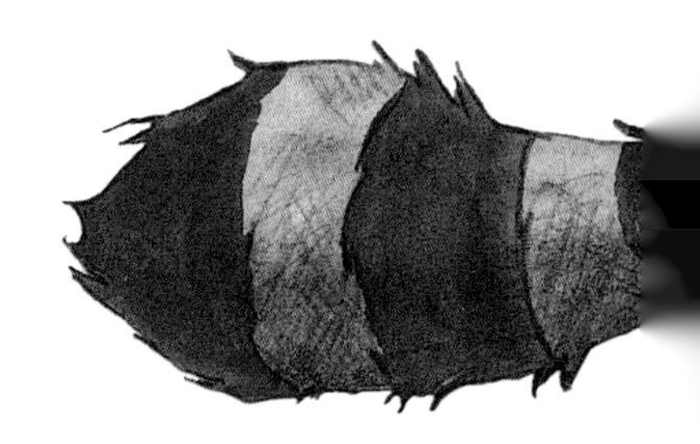

Hanna dug into the box and chose two sets of finger cymbals. She slipped her fingers through the elastic loops on the back of the cymbals.

She clanged the cymbals together until they rang out loudly.

Music made her feel even better.

She decided to look for her mom.

Her mom was working in the study.

"Mom," said Hanna. "Do you remember when I went to Lizzy's for lunch yesterday?"

"I remember," said her mom.

"Well, Lizzy was chewing with her mouth open. And when I told her she didn't have good manners, she called me a dum-dum."

"Maybe Lizzy was hoping you hadn't noticed the way she was chewing," said her mom. "Sounds like best friend trouble to me."

“She’s not my best friend,” said Hanna. “I don’t need a best friend.”

“Here,” said her mom. “Why don’t you sit at the end of my desk and draw a picture? Maybe you could give the picture to Lizzy and be friends again.”

Hanna chose a large sheet of paper and a bright orange crayon.

She drew a picture of Lizzy wearing a silly-looking dress. She covered the dress with orange balloons and gave Lizzy clonky shoes and wild orange hair.

It was such a silly drawing, it made Hanna laugh and laugh.

She decided she'd better not give the picture to Lizzy.

Because she wasn't finished complaining, Hanna went upstairs to check on her hamster, Octavia.

Octavia had been given her name because she liked to do everything eight times.

Hanna sat on the edge of the bed while Octavia tore a piece of newspaper into eight tiny strips.

"At school the other day," she told Octavia, "Lizzy said she might pick Tate to be her best friend instead of me."

Octavia gnawed as if she were listening carefully.

"And that's not all. Lizzy says her dog, Lulu, is smarter than you."

Octavia glared, then filled the pouches in her cheeks with eight seeds.

Hanna went to the window and looked down into Lizzy's yard next door.

Lizzy was sitting all alone on her back step.

Hanna went downstairs and out the front door. She sat all alone on her front step.

"That Lizzy," she muttered. "She makes me feel like shouting. If Mom tells me to wear a jacket, Lizzy is allowed to wear short sleeves. If I have to come in, Lizzy is allowed to stay out. Her birthday is even before mine and she gets to turn six before I do."

“What did you say?” said Lizzy. She was peeking around the corner of Hanna’s house.

“I said go away,” said Hanna. “I’m tired of having a best friend.”

"We could play again," said Lizzy. "You could wiggle my loose tooth."

"No thanks," said Hanna. "I have a loose tooth of my own. Anyway, you're mean."

"You were mean to me too," said Lizzy.

"When?"

“When the training wheels came off your bike,” said Lizzy. “You called me a baby because mine are still on.”

“Oh,” said Hanna. “I forgot about the bike.”

“You ran ahead on the way home from kindergarten too,” said Lizzy. “Even after I asked you to wait.”

“You could have run too,” said Hanna.

“You always win,” said Lizzy. “You’re a faster runner.”

“I am?” said Hanna. She thought for a moment. “So, I am good at some things and you are good at others. Maybe we can be friends after all.”

“Best friends?” said Lizzy.

“Why not?” said Hanna.

“We might argue again,” said Lizzy.

“I know,” said Hanna.

They sat on the step and thought about this.

“Do you want to play ball again?” said Lizzy.

“Not right now,” said Hanna. “Let’s play something nobody’s better at.”

“How about pretending? We could pretend to be best-friend monsters.”

“We could be monster partners,” said Hanna.
“That sounds like fun,” said Lizzy.
They went into Hanna’s house and up to her room.

Octavia was so happy to see them, she ran around her wheel eight times and did a belly flop.

Hanna and Lizzy lifted the lid of the craft table and reached inside.

They filled their arms with paper, crayons, paints and brushes and carried everything downstairs to the kitchen table.

They began to make monster masks.

Hanna and Lizzy cut and pasted and colored and painted.

While they helped each other and fixed their masks, they sang and sang. Everyone in the house could hear them.

The two best friends sang so hard, they sounded like two loud and happy crows.